TOOLS FOR TEACHERS

- **ATOS:** 0.6
- **GRL:** D
- **WORD COUNT:** 47

- **CURRICULUM CONNECTIONS:** emotions

Skills to Teach

- **HIGH-FREQUENCY WORDS:** a, are, do, gets, he, is, it, she, they, you
- **CONTENT WORDS:** feeling, feels, friends, happy, laughs, shares, smiles
- **PUNCTUATION:** periods, question marks
- **WORD STUDY:** long /e/, spelled ee (*feeling*, *feels*), spelled y (*happy*); long /o/, spelled ow (*show*); /oo/, spelled oo (*good*); /ow/, spelled ow (*how*)
- **TEXT TYPE:** information report

Before Reading Activities

- Read the title and give a simple statement of the main idea.
- Have students "walk" though the book and talk about what they see in the pictures.
- Introduce new vocabulary by having students predict the first letter and locate the word in the text.
- Discuss any unfamiliar concepts that are in the text.

After Reading Activities

Talk with children about different emotions. Talk about the signs of happiness. Ask the children to act out something that makes them happy. Maybe it is taking part in their favorite activity, sport, or craft. Maybe it is being with a friend. Or sharing a toy, idea, or joke. Discuss their answers as a group.

Tadpole Books are published by Jump!, 5357 Penn Avenue South, Minneapolis, MN 55419, www.jumplibrary.com

Copyright ©2019 Jump! International copyright reserved in all countries. No part of this book may be reproduced in any form without written permission from the publisher.

Editor: Jenna Trnka **Designer:** Anna Peterson

Photo Credits: drbimages/iStock, cover; ostill/Shutterstock, 1; Tomwang112/iStock, 2–3, 16tm; Inti St Clair/Getty, 4–5, 16tr, 16br; Vinicius Tupinamba/Shutterstock, 6–7 (boy); iofoto/Shutterstock, 6–7 (paper); CasarsaGuru/iStock, 8–9, 16bl; 3445128471/Shutterstock, 10–11, 16bm; wavebreakmedia/Shutterstock, 12–13, 16tl; kali9/iStock, 14–15.

Library of Congress Cataloging-in-Publication Data
Names: Nilsen, Genevieve, author.
Title: Happy / by Genevieve Nilsen.
Description: Tadpole Edition. | Minneapolis, MN : Jump!, Inc., (2018) | Series: Emotions | Includes index.
Identifiers: LCCN 2018007769 (print) | LCCN 2017061688 (ebook) | ISBN 9781624969515 (ebook) | ISBN 9781624969492 (hardcover : alk. paper) | ISBN 9781624969508 (pbk.)
Subjects: LCSH: Happiness. | Emotions.
Classification: LCC BF575.H27 (print) | LCC BF575.H27 N55 2018 (ebook) | DDC 152.4/2—dc23
LC record available at https://lccn.loc.gov/2018007769

EMOTIONS

HAPPY

by Genevieve Nilsen

TABLE OF CONTENTS

tadpole
books

HAPPY

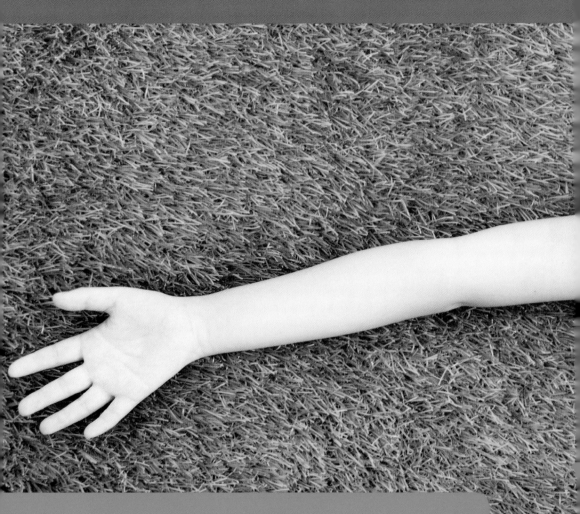

Happy is a feeling.

She feels happy.

smile

He smiles.

He laughs.

Spelling A+ Name: David

state State   door door   paper paper

word word   floor floor   school

apple apple   roof roof   road road

house house   tree tree   city city

mouse mouse   star star   mail mail

table table   moon moon   stamp stamp

                     earth earth   street street

pencil pencil

He gets a good grade.

He feels happy.

picture

She paints a picture.

She feels happy.

He shares.

He feels happy.

They are friends.

They feel happy.

Are you happy?

How do you show it?

WORDS TO KNOW

friends

happy

laughs

paints

shares

smiles

INDEX